LITTLE SIMON

An imprint of Simon & Schuster Children's Publishing Division

1230 Avenue of the Americas, New York, New York 10020

First Little Simon hardcover edition August 2019

Copyright © 2019 by New York City Ballet Incorporated

All rights reserved, including the right of reproduction in whole or in part in any form.

LITTLE SIMON is a registered trademark of Simon & Schuster, Inc., and associated colophon is a trademark of Simon & Schuster, Inc. For information about special discounts for bulk purchases, please contact Simon & Schuster Special Sales at 1-866-506-1949 or business@simonandschuster.com.

The Simon & Schuster Speakers Bureau can bring authors to your live event.

For more information or to book an event contact the Simon & Schuster Speakers Bureau at 1-866-248-3049 or visit our website at www.simonspeakers.com.

Lettering by Angela Navarra

Designed by Chani Yammer

Manufactured in China 0619 SCP

2 4 6 8 10 9 7 5 3 1

This book has been cataloged with the Library of Congress.

ISBN 978-1-4814-5833-7 (hc)

ISBN 978-1-4814-5834-4 (eBook)

SWAN LAKE

LITTLE SIMON

New York   London   Toronto   Sydney   New Delhi

It was Prince Siegfried's twenty-first birthday, and the castle was alive with joy and laughter as the court jester entertained the party guests.

While the crowd was celebrating, the queen arrived with a royal to-do.
She made her way to her son to give him a birthday present of a magnificent
golden crossbow.

The thrill of the gift was blunted for the prince, however, when his mother said, "You are now twenty-one, my son. It is time for you to find a bride because it is your royal duty to marry." The prince sadly hung his head. To him, marriage meant the end of his days as a carefree boy.

Prince Siegfried's best friend, Benno, understood how the prince felt, so he tried to cheer him up by raising a toast and leading a spirited dance—but the prince remained glum.

When the sun began to set, a flock of swans flew overhead. This gave Benno an idea. He handed the prince his new crossbow and called for a hunting trip to the swans' lake. But Prince Siegfried waved his friends away, still lost in sadness at his mother's command to marry soon.

It was only after his friends set off that the prince had a change of heart. Maybe a hunt would cheer him up after all. He picked up the bow and left for the lake. When he stepped from the forest into a clearing, he came upon a flock of swans. To his amazement, one of the swans turned into the loveliest young woman he'd ever seen, right before his eyes.

The woman recoiled from him in fear, and Prince Siegfried quickly put down his bow to show he meant her no harm. Her name was Odette, and she was the queen of the swans.

Odette explained that she and her friends had been placed under a spell by a wicked sorcerer named von Rothbart. By day they were doomed to live as swans, but for a few hours each night they were allowed to return to their human form. There was only one way to lift the curse: Someone who had never loved before must swear his love to Odette and marry her.

The Swan Queen had barely finished her tale when a figure sprang from the shadows of the forest, and Prince Siegfried found himself face-to-face with von Rothbart. The prince raised his bow to destroy the evil sorcerer, but Odette pleaded with him to hold his fire. If von Rothbart died before the spell was broken, the curse could never be undone, and she would be doomed to be a swan forever.

Von Rothbart slunk back into the forest, his cape flowing behind him ominously. The clearing then filled with Odette's friends, who danced beautifully, though sadly, since they understood their fate. While they danced, the prince and the Swan Queen fell in love under a starry sky.

Filled with love, Odette and her friends twirled, leaped, and glided gracefully in the light of the moon.

As dawn lifted the dark of night, von Rothbart's power summoned the swans back to the glistening lake. Prince Siegfried pledged his true love to Odette and promised to hurry back to marry her and finally break the evil spell. He watched helplessly when the arms that had embraced him turned back into the feathered wings of a swan.

The very next day, the queen held a grand ball at the castle. The court jester and his three apprentices, along with dancers from around the world, amazed the crowd.

The queen had invited six princesses to the ball, and she hoped one of them would be a good match for the prince. The prince dutifully danced with each princess to please his mother, but while he danced he could think only of Odette, his beloved Swan Queen.

All the dancers were swirling around the ballroom when two late arrivals caught Prince Siegfried's eye. They appeared to be a knight and his daughter, who was dressed in a shimmering black gown and a glittering tiara. The prince's heart skipped a beat and then soared. She was Odette! He sailed across the floor, swept her into his arms, and joyfully danced for the rest of the night.

But it was all a wicked trick. The knight was von Rothbart in disguise, and the young beauty the prince thought was Odette was actually Odile, von Rothbart's daughter. Von Rothbart had magically disguised Odile to look exactly like the prince's true love, Odette.

The trick worked. The prince was fooled. He didn't recognize von Rothbart, nor did he sense Odette's frantic attempt to alert him to the evil plan. The prince pledged his love to the young woman he thought was Odette, and he announced to the queen and court that he would like to take her hand in marriage.

As soon as the prince made his proclamation, von Rothbart stepped forward in triumph to reveal that Odile was not Odette. Both father and daughter laughed fiendishly when Prince Siegfried realized with horror that he had broken his vow to his one true love.

Because of his mistake, the spell could now not be broken.
Odette and her friends were cursed to remain swans until
the end of their days. Everyone at the castle was aghast, and
Prince Siegfried fled to search for his Swan Queen.

Prince Siegfried reached the lake to find a heartbroken Odette being comforted by her fellow swans. With anguish, the prince explained that he had been tricked and that he had not meant to betray her. He begged her for forgiveness.

Odette knew in her heart that Prince Siegfried was being truthful, and she forgave him. Their love was true.

When von Rothbart arrived at the lake to claim victory, he saw that the love between Odette and Prince Siegfried was pure and strong. He could never break their bonds of love. He flew into a rage and crumpled to the ground in defeat: True love would never die, and the prince would not marry Odile.

But the spell still could not be broken,
and the curse could not be lifted. Odette
would remain a swan forever.

After a long night, dawn came, and once more the spell pulled Odette and the swans back to the lake. Her outstretched arms turned once again to feathered wings. Prince Siegfried reached out for her one last time, but he knew when she slipped away that he would remain in love, but alone, forevermore.

New York City Ballet's

SWAN LAKE

Fun Facts

- Each performance features more than 70 NYCB dancers, 21 children from the School of American Ballet (the official school of NYCB), and 59 musicians in the NYCB orchestra.

- More than 140 costumes are worn by the cast.

- The ballerina who dances the lead role in *Swan Lake* portrays two characters: Odette, the Swan Queen, and Odile, the evil impostor pretending to be the Swan Queen.

- Act One features 1 golden crossbow, a birthday gift from the queen to her son, Prince Siegfried, and 20 drinking goblets used in a toast to the prince for the occasion.

- There are four little swans, or cygnets, who perform the famous linked-arm dance in Act Two.

- The ballerina performing the role of Odile must perform 32 fouettés, which are fast turns on one leg, during the iconic pas de deux.

- In addition to Odette, the last act of the ballet features 28 swans: 20 wearing white tutus and 8 wearing black tutus, with each tutu made from 15 yards of tulle.

- The Danish painter Per Kirkeby created 5 exquisitely painted backdrops for this production.

Swan Lake, now considered one of the most popular ballets of all time, was not well received at its premiere, which took place at Moscow's Bolshoi Theater on March 4, 1877, in a production choreographed by Julius Reisinger.

Drawing inspiration from a folktale about a wicked sorcerer who turns young women into birds, the score for the four-act ballet was created by the famed Russian composer Peter Ilyitch Tschaikovsky, who would go on to write scores for *The Sleeping Beauty* (1890) and *The Nutcracker* (1892). In 1895, a few years after Tschaikovsky's death, a new production of *Swan Lake* was created with choreography by Marius Petipa for acts one and three and choreography by Lev Ivanov for acts two and four. This time the production, which opened at St. Petersburg's Mariinsky Theater on January 27, 1895, became a great success, and the version by Petipa and Ivanov would become the basis for most productions of *Swan Lake* that followed.

George Balanchine, one of the cofounders of **New York City Ballet**, created a one-act version of *Swan Lake* in 1951, which combined mostly new choreography with several of Ivanov's dances from act two of the ballet. In 1996, NYCB's then Ballet Master in Chief Peter Martins staged a full-length *Swan Lake* for Copenhagen's Royal Danish Ballet, which featured sets and costumes designed by the acclaimed Danish painter Per Kirkeby. In 1999, this production of *Swan Lake*, which incorporates choreography by Martins, Petipa, Ivanov, and Balanchine, entered the repertory of New York City Ballet.

Swan Lake

Music by **Peter Ilyitch Tschaikovsky**

Choreography by **Peter Martins**
after **Marius Petipa**, **Lev Ivanov**, and **George Balanchine**

Scenery and costumes* by **Per Kirkeby**
(*Costumes based on original designs by **Per Kirkeby** and **Kirsten Lund Nielsen**)

Costumes realized by **Barbara Matera**

Lighting by **Mark Stanley**

Premiere: October 27, 1996, Royal Danish Ballet,
Royal Theater, Copenhagen
New York City Ballet Premiere: April 29, 1999, New York State Theater, New York

Learn more at **nycballet.com**.